Claire

and the
Water Wish

For C.H.

Kids Can Press acknowledges the financial support of the Government of Ontario, through the Ontario Media Development Corporation's Ontario Book Initiative; the Ontario Arts Council; the Canada Council for the Arts; and the Government of Canada, through the BPIDP, for our publishing activity.

Published in Canada by
Kids Can Press Ltd.
29 Birch Avenue
Toronto, ON M4V 1E2

Published in the U.S. by
Kids Can Press Ltd.
2250 Military Road
Tonawanda, NY 14150

www.kidscanpress.com

Edited by Karen Li
Designed by Kathleen Gray
Printed and bound in Singapore

The hardcover edition of this book is smyth sewn casebound.
The paperback edition of this book is limp sewn with drawn-on cover.

CM 09 0 9 8 7 6 5 4 3 2 1
CM PA 09 0 9 8 7 6 5 4 3 2 1

Library and Archives Canada Cataloguing in Publication

Poon, Janice
     Claire and the water wish / Janice Poon.

Target audience: For ages 7–10.
ISBN 978-1-55453-381-7 (bound). ISBN 978-1-55453-382-4 (pbk.)

1. Pollution—Comic books, strips, etc. I. Title.

PS8631.O638C533 2009   j741.5'971   C2008-903252-7

Kids Can Press is a *f,©rJs*™ Entertainment company

Claire

and the
Water Wish

Written and illustrated by
JANICE POON

Kids Can Press

Dear Diary:

I can't believe summer's over. Moving to the country has been awesome (especially since I met Jet, my new best friend). But now that September's here, I've been thinking a lot about my old friends at Bigville Public School. Right now I bet they're all at the mall shopping for new clothes. I'm missing all that fun.

Things are so different here. Dear diary, do you think I'll make friends at my new school? I don't care about being popular, but I wonder if I'll fit in.

Claire

7

Claire's my new neighbor. She was on TV this summer. She rescued her mom from a kidnapper.

I like your backpack. Is that a TinkiToy? You should hang it on your lunch box. See mine?

That's cute. I don't use a lunch box. At Bigville Public, everyone carries lunch in their backpack.

Everyone *here* uses a lunch box.

9

Dear Diary:

School here is better than I imagined. Everyone's pretty friendly, and I really like Ms. Beene, my teacher. I hope I do okay in her class. I don't want her to think I'm an idiot — which I'm not.

Jet is totally obsessed with the camera contest. That's all she talks about now. There are only ten prizes being awarded in the whole school district, but she's positive she's going to win one. That's Jet, no doubt!

Claire

Dear Diary:

Big news! Jet won the contest — and the camera! She wrote an essay on how the family farm is like an endangered species. Ms. Beene always says to write about what you know, and it worked! No wonder Jet's been so sneaky lately. She never showed me her essay or anything before she handed it in. She said I've been too busy with Sky. What's that supposed to mean?

Claire

Stop. You're driving me *crrrrrazy* with that camera.

Whoa. Not that angry.

Give me that thing. See how you like "candid shots."

But you can borrow my camera 'til tomorrow.

Are you sure?

Yes. I'm helping Mom box vegetables tonight. She's paying me so I can buy a camera bag.

A camera bag?

It's part of my new look.

34

We'd better get going on our presentation. Let's take our diorama to my place and work on it together over the weekend.

I can get my Dad to drive me in on Saturday.

Okay, Jet?

I can't. I promised Tabby and Erica I'd take some pictures of them.

Forget it.
I'm sure Tabby and Erica
will want tons and tons
of pictures.

Dear Diary:

Things have gotten so mixed up ever since Jet won that camera. Now she only wants to hang with the popular kids. I think they're just using her to get pictures of themselves. Maybe tomorrow when we're at the market — where there aren't any cliques — we'll have fun together like we used to.

Claire

GOOD OLD **FUN** AHEAD

TO MARKET

That's where they have some really cool stuff.

I hope we can find some cute lunch boxes.

I thought you said lunch boxes were for kindergarten.

Oh, I love it.

It has compartments.

Excellent for my attachments if I get any.

Denim is dull. This bag has "flair."

Yeah, like an emergency flare. We'll never lose you in the snow with that thing around your neck.

You're serious ...

Claire, this is the new me. You're too busy hanging out with Sky to notice.

First we get a branch that looks like a wishbone. Like this!

Now what? I thought you said it only works for water witches.

I am a water witch!

You're kidding.

Dear Diary:

Guess what! We got an A+ for our diorama! It turned out fantastic. (No thanks to Jet.) Tabby and Erica were GREEN with envy.

To celebrate, Sky's dad has invited us to Lovesick Lake next Sunday for their Wild Earth Festival. It's a fundraiser to help pay for the community's new water well. Mom and Dad said we worked so hard on our project we deserve to go, and Jet's mom agreed. I can't wait! I'm going to take my whole science kit so I can make notes on new species for my scrapbook.

Claire

She's driving everyone nuts.

There's no harm in it.

It's not like she's taking pictures of nature. She wants to be a fashion photographer. How boring.

It's her way of making friends.

Shallow friends who just want to be models or something.

Oh, Claire, it's just a phase. She's having fun ...

C'mon inside, Grumpy. There's a drumming session you're gonna love. And lunch is almost ready.

PING!

We wanted to go after them. But by then I had run out of beads, so we couldn't find our way back to the road.

But we found this clearing and decided to try to send a sign to Ranger Rhonda.

It must have been so scary.

But so fantastic because we discovered who is polluting Sky's lake.

Dad!

Promise me that you will stay out of these dangerous situations.

Claire, again, I must remind you. Apprehending criminals is better left to the police.

And that goes double for you two.

Dear Diary:

It's been so exciting. The people from the newspaper and TV have been calling us nonstop for interviews. I've promised to sew every single jewel back onto Jet's camera bag so she can wear it on TV.

Dad is taking us into the city tomorrow so we can go to court and hear the verdict. We are learning a lot about how the justice system works. Sky is thinking of becoming a lawyer, and now Jet wants to be a newspaper photographer. I think I'll stick with zoology. It's not as beastly.

Claire

Jet's Crafts for Future Famous Photographers

Taking photos is fun. But don't just let them sit in an album or on your computer. Make cool stuff like this and share it with your friends.

You probably have a lot of the materials you will need at home. Remember to get permission to use them.

Tiny Photo Tags

Hang these on your school bag or lunch box or anywhere you want mini pictures of your friends.

These little framed photos are made with metal rim key tags found anywhere keys are cut and at office supply stores. Look for ball chain at hardware stores.

YOU WILL NEED

two photos

a 25-cent coin

a pencil

scissors

a paint brush

a 3.175 cm (1 1/4 in.) round metal rim key tag

two 7 cm (2 3/4 in.) lengths of ball chain

white glue

water

a small container

a plastic spoon

1. Choose an area of the first photo you wish to put on your tag. Using the coin as a guide, trace a circle around that area and cut it out.

2. Position the photo on the key tag and trim if necessary to allow the key ring to move freely in the hole.

3. Prepare glue mixture by stirring four spoons of glue and one spoon of water together in a small bowl. Brush one side of the key tag with the glue mixture and immediately press the photo on top, centering it on the tag. Allow to dry for 5 minutes, then apply another coat of glue mixture over the photo and up to the metal rim.

4. Squeeze a thin line of white glue between the photo and the rim. Using a toothpick, position the ball chain into a ring around the photo. Allow to dry, then brush liberally with another coat of glue mixture. Allow to dry overnight.

5. Repeat on the reverse side.

Claire's Jewel Case Frame

Recycle an old CD case to make a bedazzled frame for your favorite photo.

YOU WILL NEED

a discarded CD case with CD
white glue
a small container
assorted beads, buttons and jewels
tweezers

1. Remove CD and album cover from the case and set aside.

2. Pour a small amount of white glue into the container. One at a time, dip beads and jewels into the glue and position them around the border of the case, using the tweezers if necessary. Leave the center area undecorated so your photo will show through. Set aside to dry.

3. In the meantime, select a photo or a picture from a magazine. Using the album cover as a guide, trace a square on the image, then cut it out.

4. Place the trimmed picture in the case and snap closed.

Accordion Photo Album

You can display LOTS of pictures in Claire's Jewel Case Frame by making this accordion photo album.

YOU WILL NEED

Claire's Jewel Case Frame
the discarded CD
a pencil
2 sheets colored construction paper
scissors
5 photos with a 13 cm x 13 cm (5 in. x 5 in.) image area
a glue stick
1 60-cm (23-in.) length of ribbon

1. Using the CD as a guide, trace four circles on the colored paper, and cut them out. Do the same with the photos, centering the circles on the areas that you like the most.

2. Line up the CD and the colored paper circles so they are side by side without overlapping.

3. Run the glue stick along the length of one side of the ribbon.

4. Place the ribbon, glue side down, on the CD and paper circles, connecting them along their middles. Trim off any excess ribbon.

5. Apply glue to the ribbon, the CD and the colored paper circles. Place your photo circles on top of the CD and the paper circles, sandwiching the ribbon. Set aside to dry.

6. When the glue has dried, you can write a fun description on the colored paper backing of each photo. Place the CD back into the case, photo side up, and press to snap into place. Accordion-fold the photos on top of each other and snap the case closed.

Happy crafting, and *see* you next time!

When Sam and friends are on the case, adventure is never far behind.

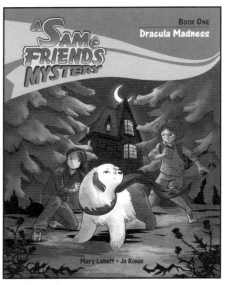

Sam has moved to town, and she's no ordinary dog! This canine detective with *attitude* has a nose for trouble and an appetite for adventure.

Sam meets ten-year-old Jennie — her new friend and dog walker — who has the special ability to "hear" Sam's thoughts. Together, they find the perfect setting for a mystery adventure: the spookiest house in town. *Why* is the house always dark? *How* come the owner never lets anyone inside? *What* could he be hiding?

Dracula Madness
A Sam and Friends Mystery
Written by Mary Labatt   Illustrated by Jo Rioux
Hardcover 978-1-55453-418-0
Paperback 978-1-55337-303-2